Jacob
~ and the ~
Polar Bears

By Janet Graber

Illustrated by
Sandra Salzillo-Shields

Moon Mountain
PUBLISHING

North Kingstown, Rhode Island

First edition.

Library of Congress Cataloging-in-Publication Data

Graber, Janet.
    Jacob and the polar bears / by Janet Graber ; illustrated by
Sandra Salzillo-Shields.
        p. cm.
Summary: All one hundred and seventy-two naughty polar
bears climb off of Jacob's new second-hand pajamas in the
middle of the night and escape for a swim in an icy winter pond.
    ISBN 1-931659-00-1 (alk. paper)
    [1. Pajamas—Fiction. 2. Polar bear—Fiction. 3. Bears—Fiction.
4. Humorous stories.] I. Salzillo-Shields, Sandra, ill. II. Title.
    PZ7.G7488 Jac 2002
    [Fic]—dc21

                                    2002002462

Moon Mountain Publishing
80 Peachtree Road
North Kingstown, RI 02852
www.moonmountainpub.com

Printed in South Korea

10 9 8 7 6 5 4 3 2 1

For Richard—
With love and gratitude for your
unwavering faith as time goes by. J.G.

To my husband, Robin, always and forever,
and to my daughter, Carly, with much love. S.S-S.

Jacob and the Polar Bears

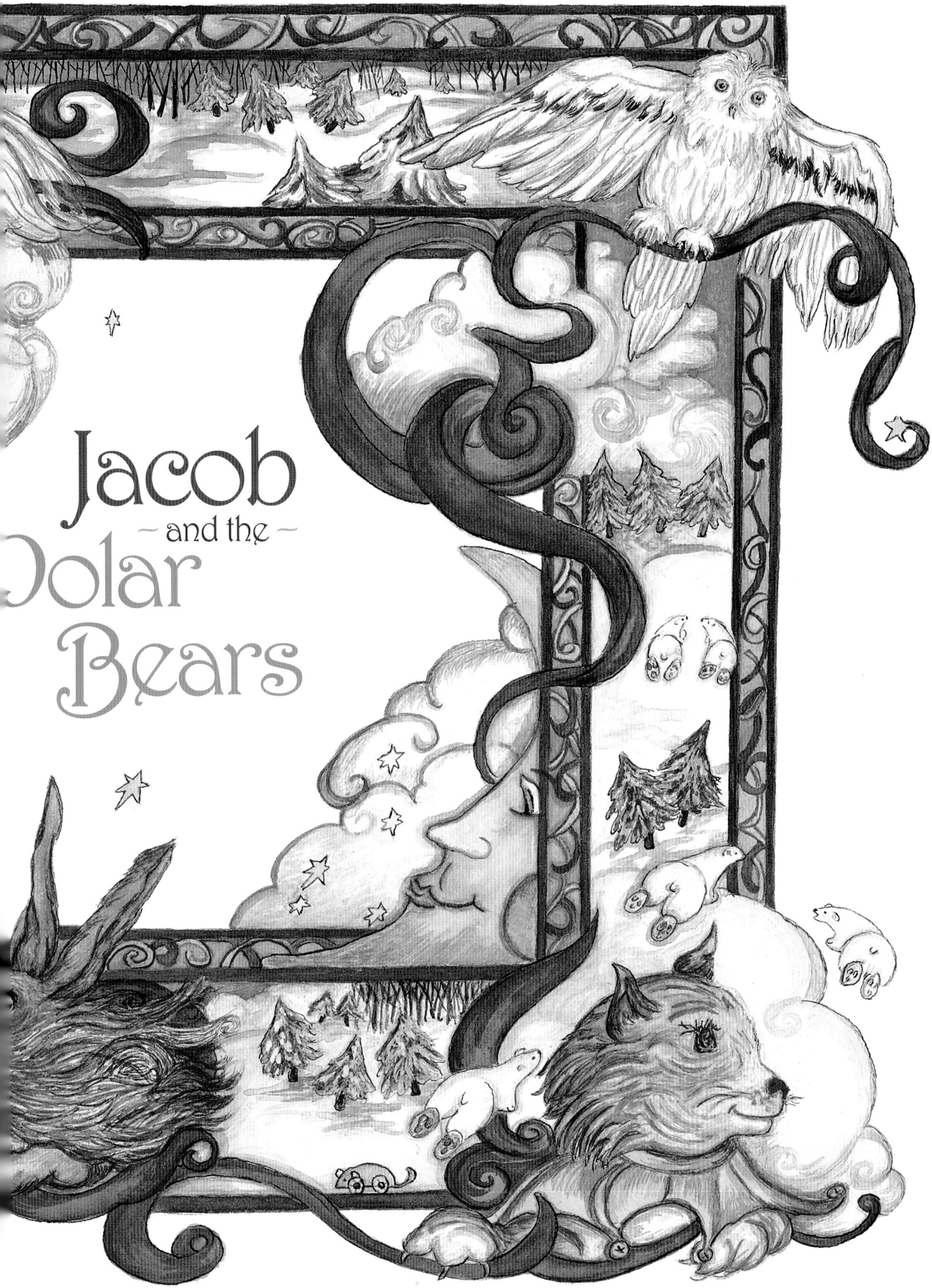

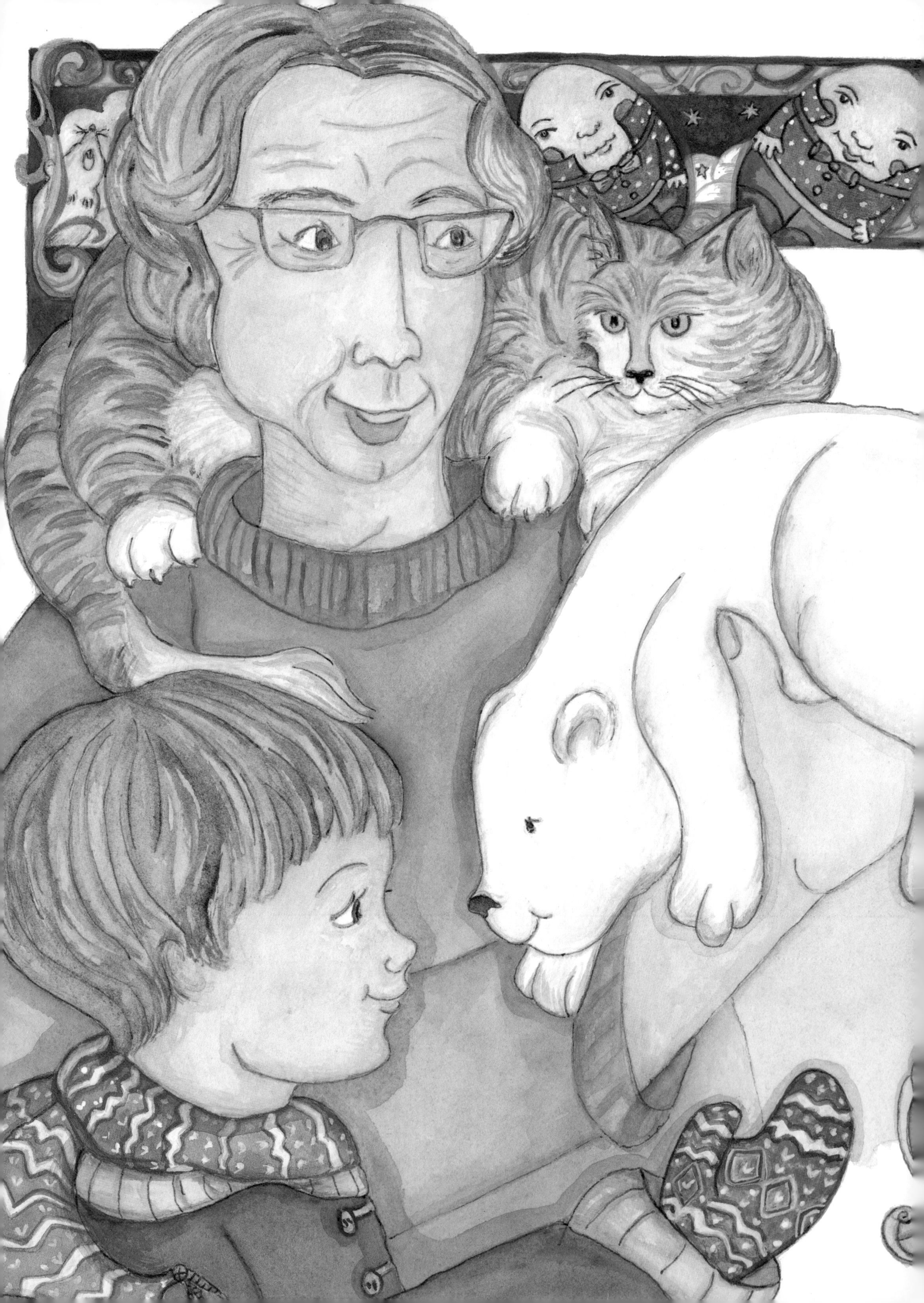

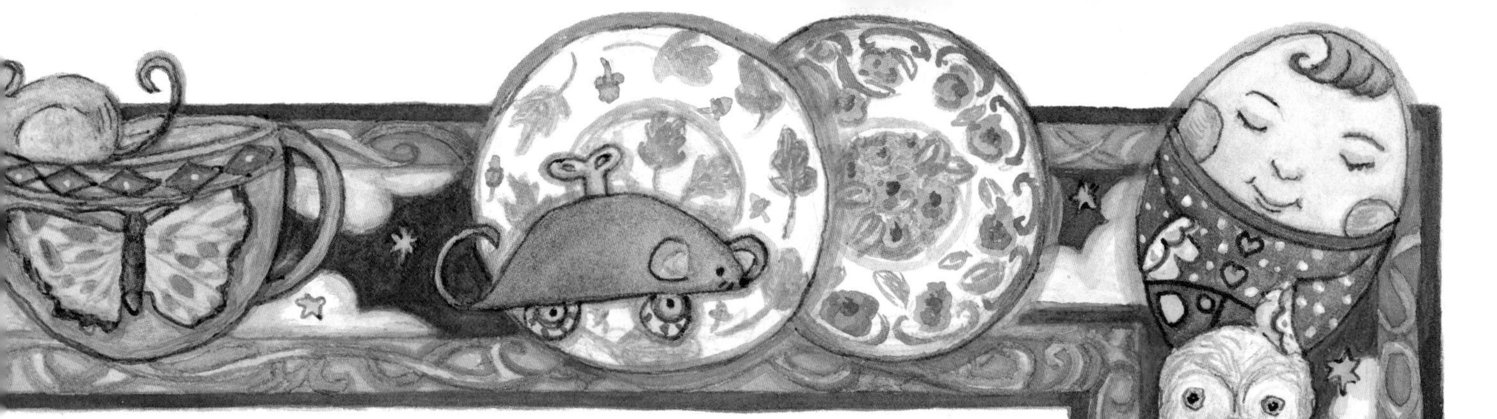

"Are they very special pajamas?" Jacob asked.

"Indeed they are," said Mrs. Thrifty of the Good-as-New shop. She held the green pajamas, decorated with one-hundred-and-seventy-two white polar bears, against Jacob's chest.

"They'll do nicely, thank you," Jacob's mom said, counting out coins from her purse.

"But beware, Jacob," said Mrs. Thrifty with a twinkle in her eye. "These bears can be naughty." She reached high on a dusty shelf for a dingy, stuffed polar bear, hidden among moldy furs, top hats, and china bowls. "King will watch over the naughty polar bears while you sleep."

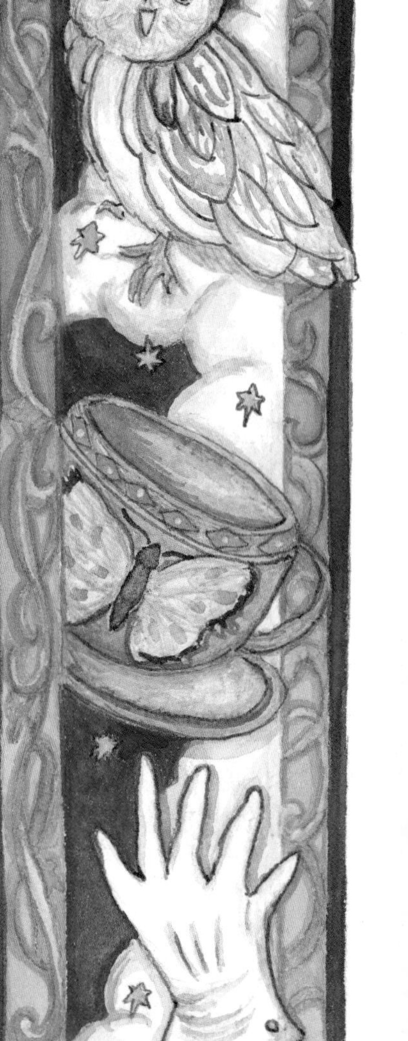

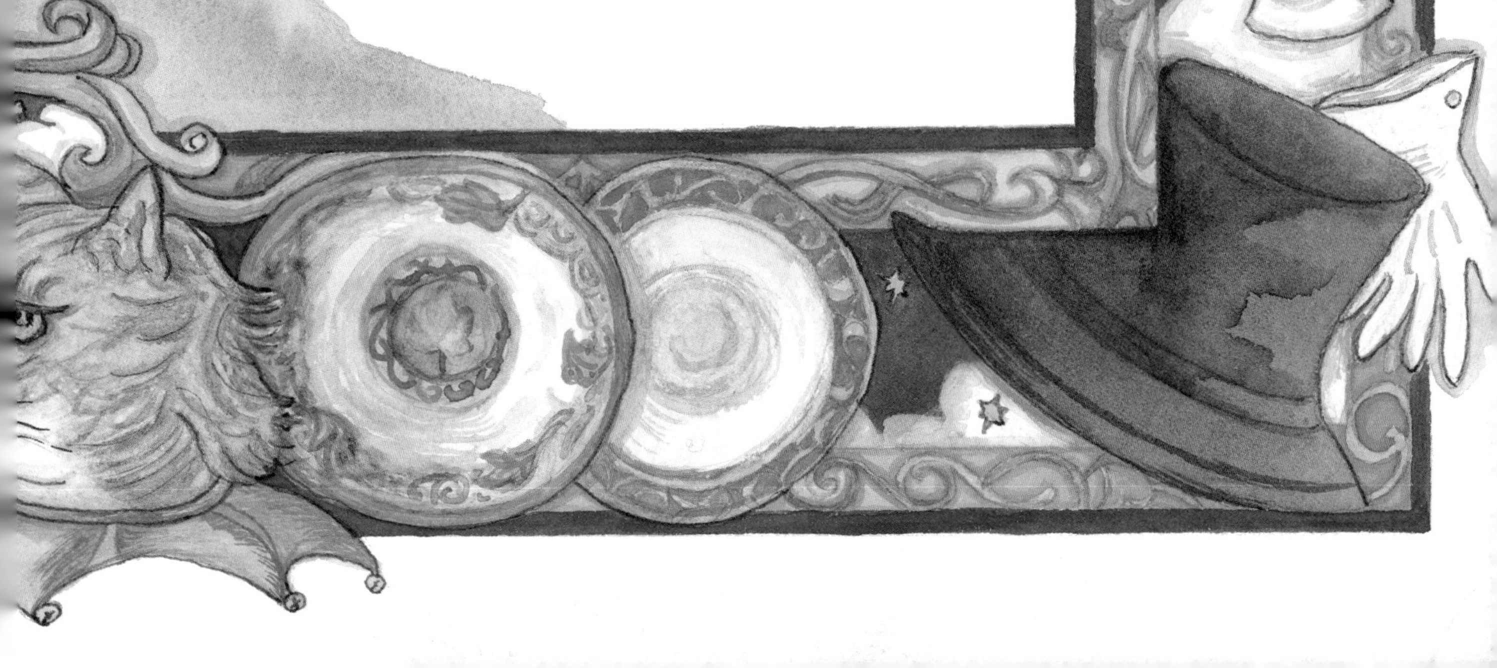

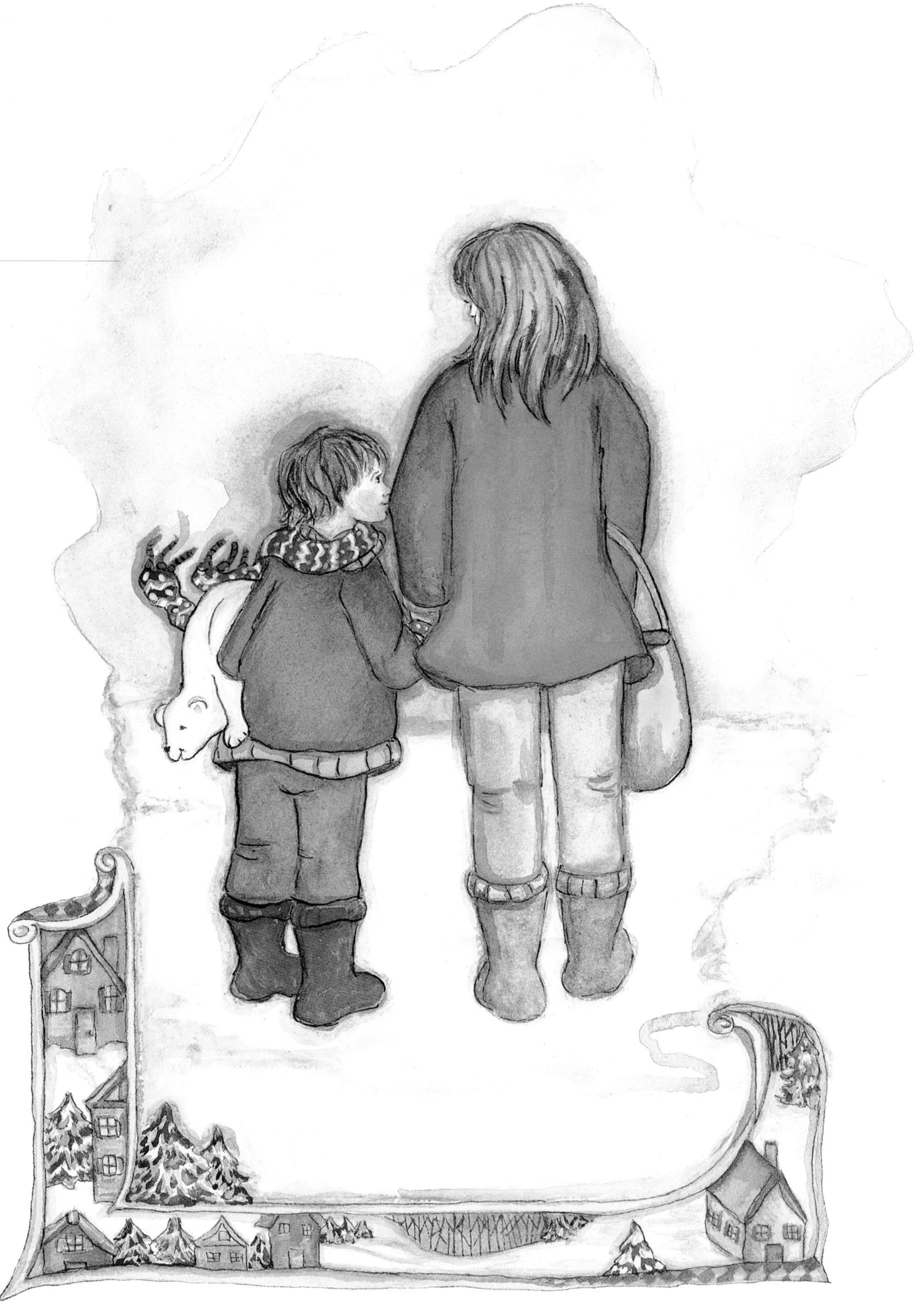

Jacob's mom carried the very special pajamas in a
paper sack, Jacob carried King tucked under his arm,
and they crunched through the snowy streets, over
the icy bridge, and home.

When it was time for bed, Jacob put on his
good-as-new pajamas and placed King on his dresser
to watch over the naughty polar bears.

"Sweet dreams," Jacob's mom said, and she
kissed him goodnight.

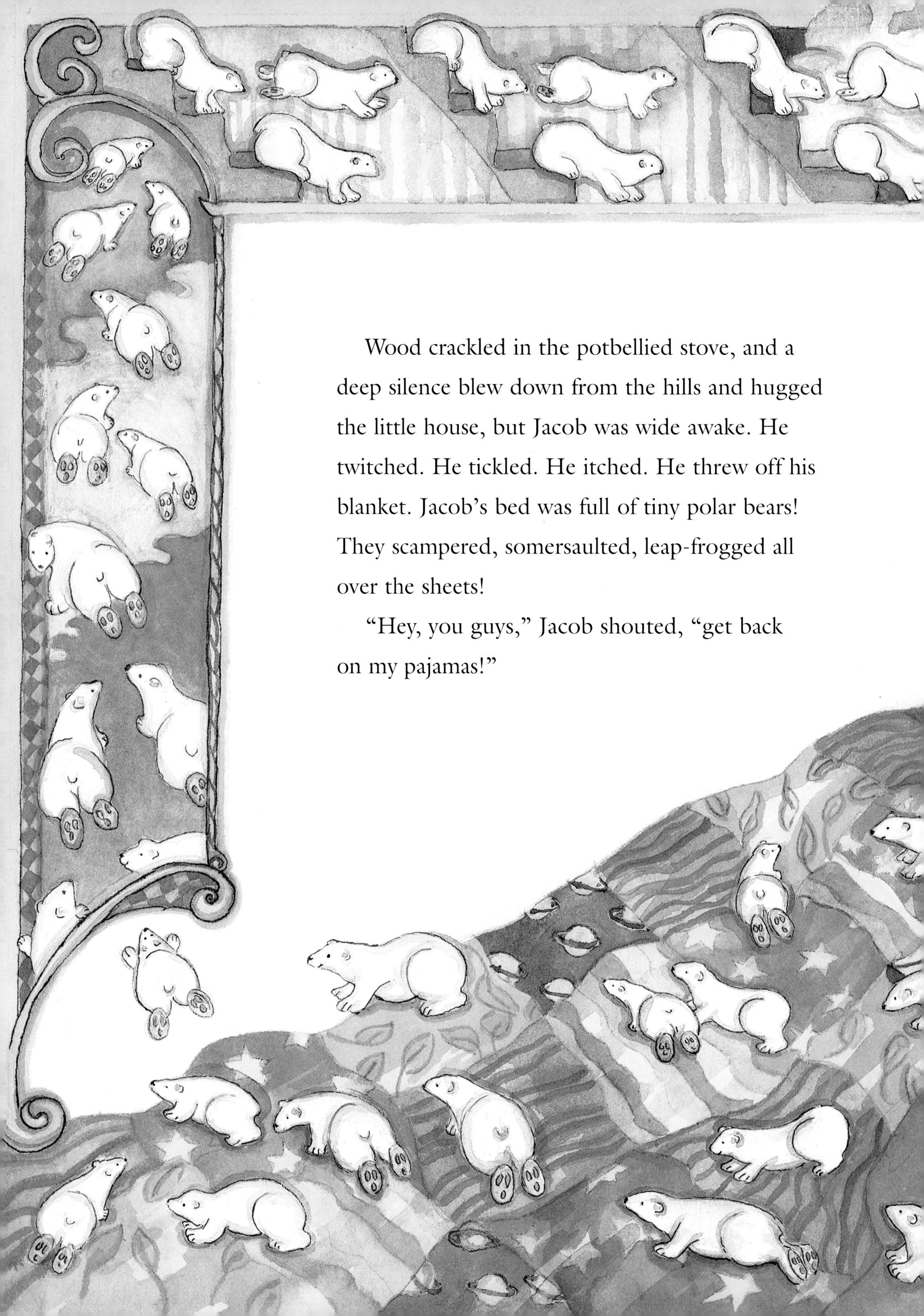

Wood crackled in the potbellied stove, and a deep silence blew down from the hills and hugged the little house, but Jacob was wide awake. He twitched. He tickled. He itched. He threw off his blanket. Jacob's bed was full of tiny polar bears! They scampered, somersaulted, leap-frogged all over the sheets!

"Hey, you guys," Jacob shouted, "get back on my pajamas!"

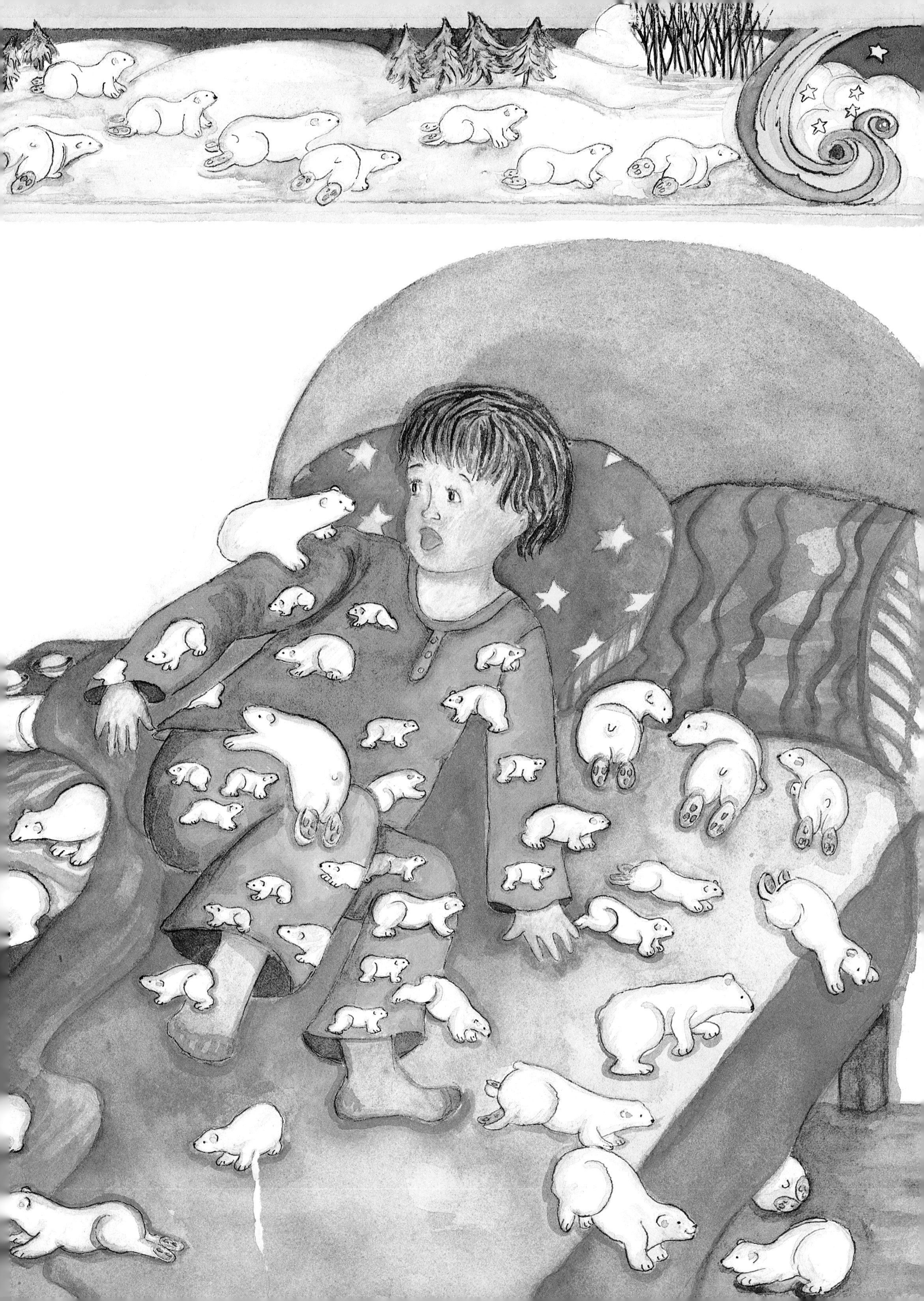

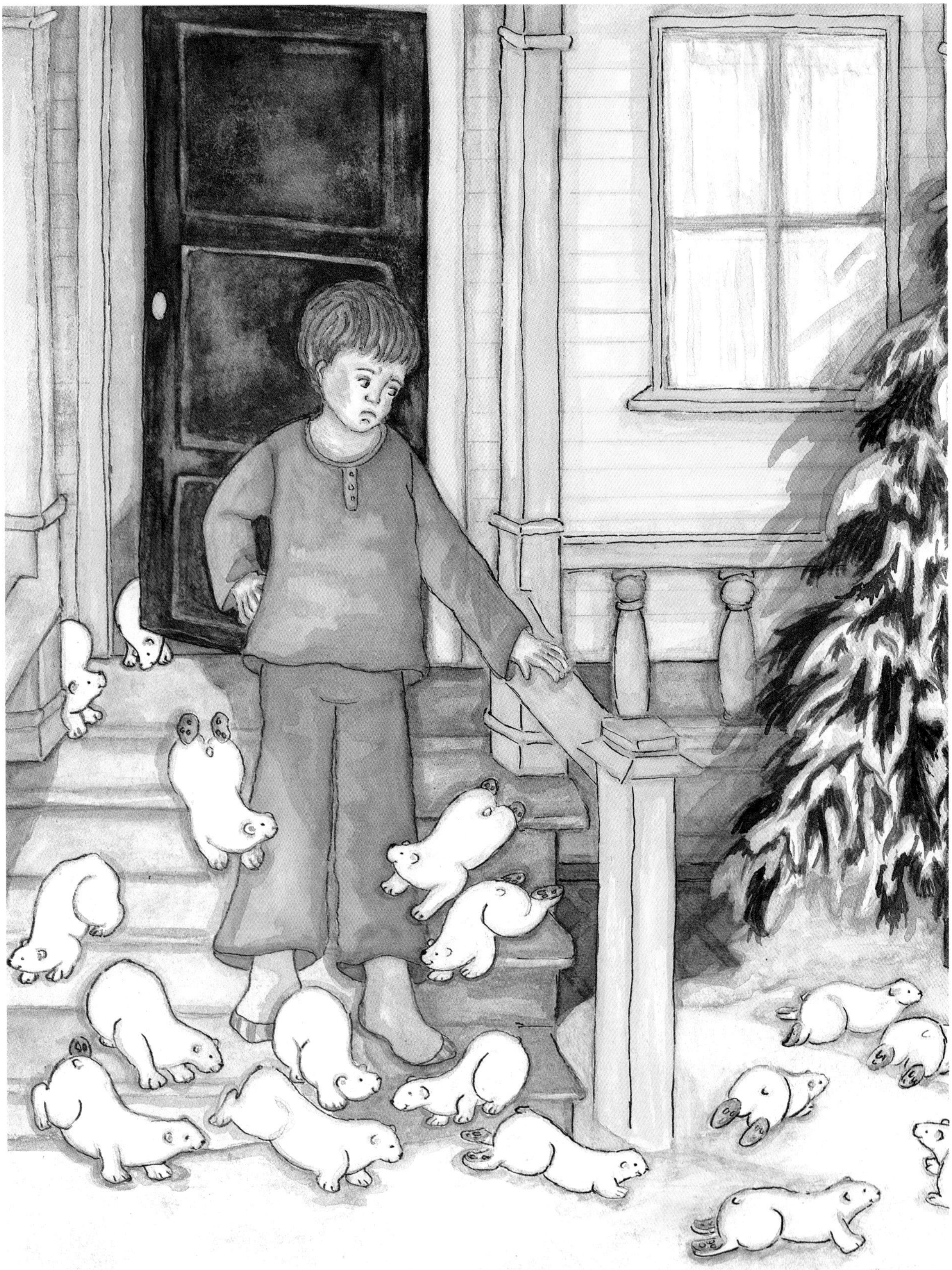

"No, we won't, won't, won't." The bears tumbled off Jacob's bed
and raced downstairs. "We're going swimming in the cold, cold
night. Swimming, swimming, swimming," sang the naughty little
polar bears in silly voices as they squeezed beneath the kitchen door.

"Oh, no," Jacob moaned. "Come back."

But the bears rolled off the porch steps and romped through the
dry, crackling cornstalks standing in the garden.

"Hey, bears," Jacob yelled, "I'm not allowed to go down to the
creek alone." Jacob's plain green pajamas flapped in the cold night air.

"Too bad, bad, bad," chanted the polar bears. "We need
to swim, swim, swim. It's what polar bears do, do, do." And
the bears bounced across the snowy meadow towards the
swimming hole.

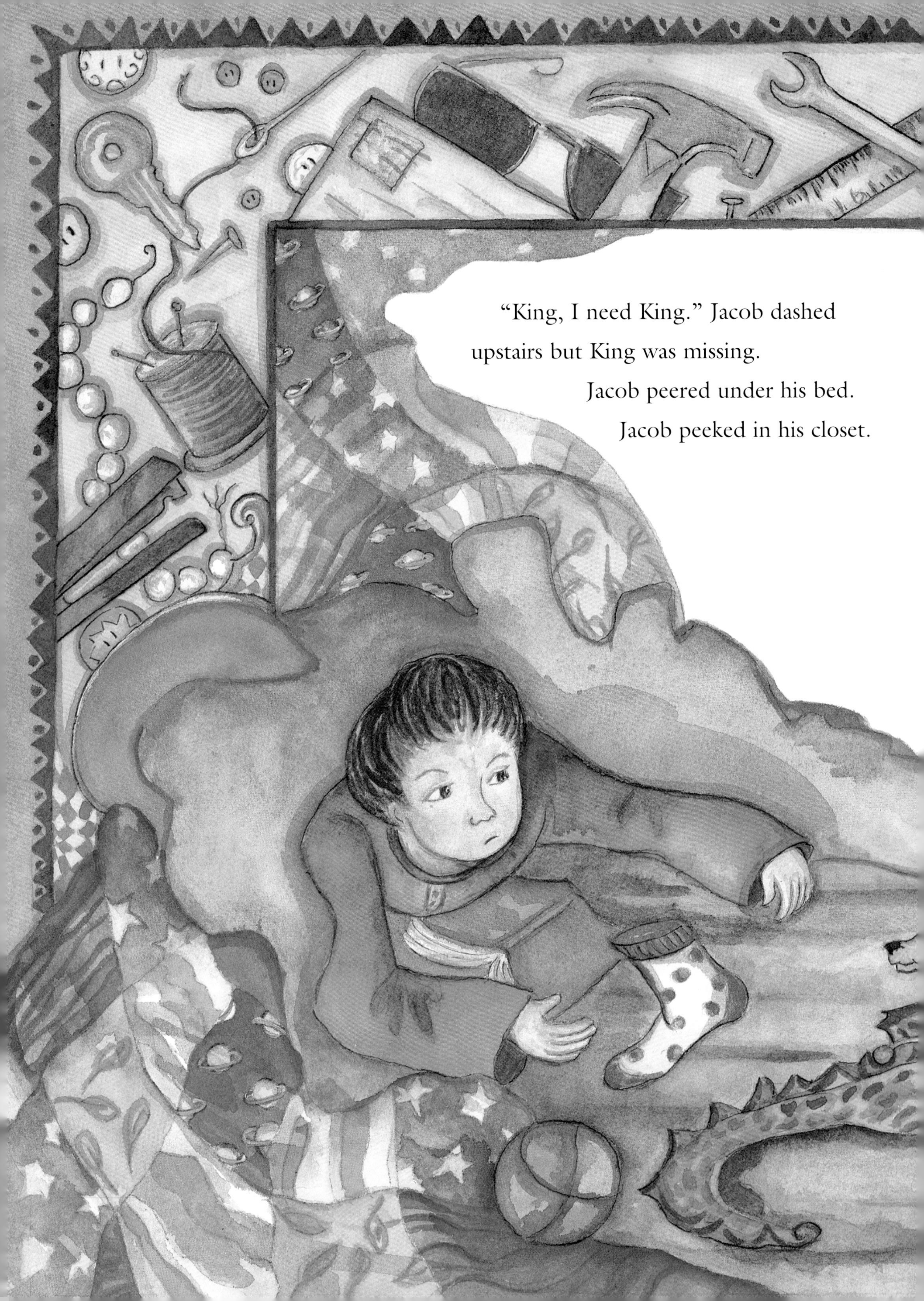

"King, I need King." Jacob dashed upstairs but King was missing.

Jacob peered under his bed.

Jacob peeked in his closet.

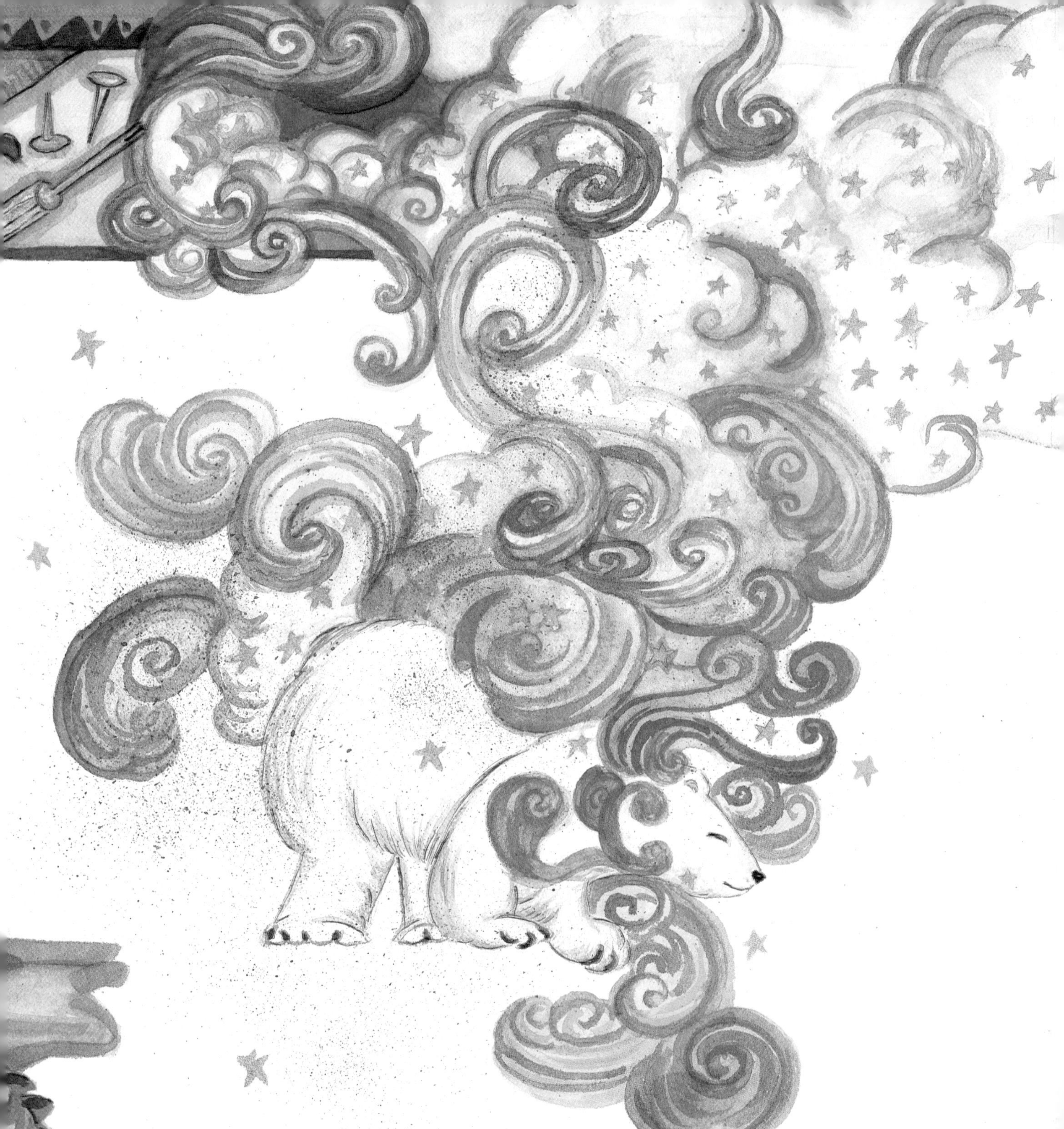

Jacob pried open his dad's toolbox. Jacob peeped in his mom's desk. Jacob pushed into his sister's room.

"Out, Jacob," she said.

Jacob poked his head into the bathroom. Water slopped in great puddles on the floor. King, grown to enormous size, was wedged in the bathtub.

"Look at me," Jacob shouted, clutching his plain green pajamas. "One-hundred-and-seventy-two polar bears have escaped to the swimming hole. Let's go!"

King blinked his beady-black eyes. King reared up on his hind legs and bumped his head on the ceiling. King shook his great furry body, and water cascaded about the room like a waterfall.

"Hurry," Jacob begged. "The swimming hole is deep and they are such tiny bears."

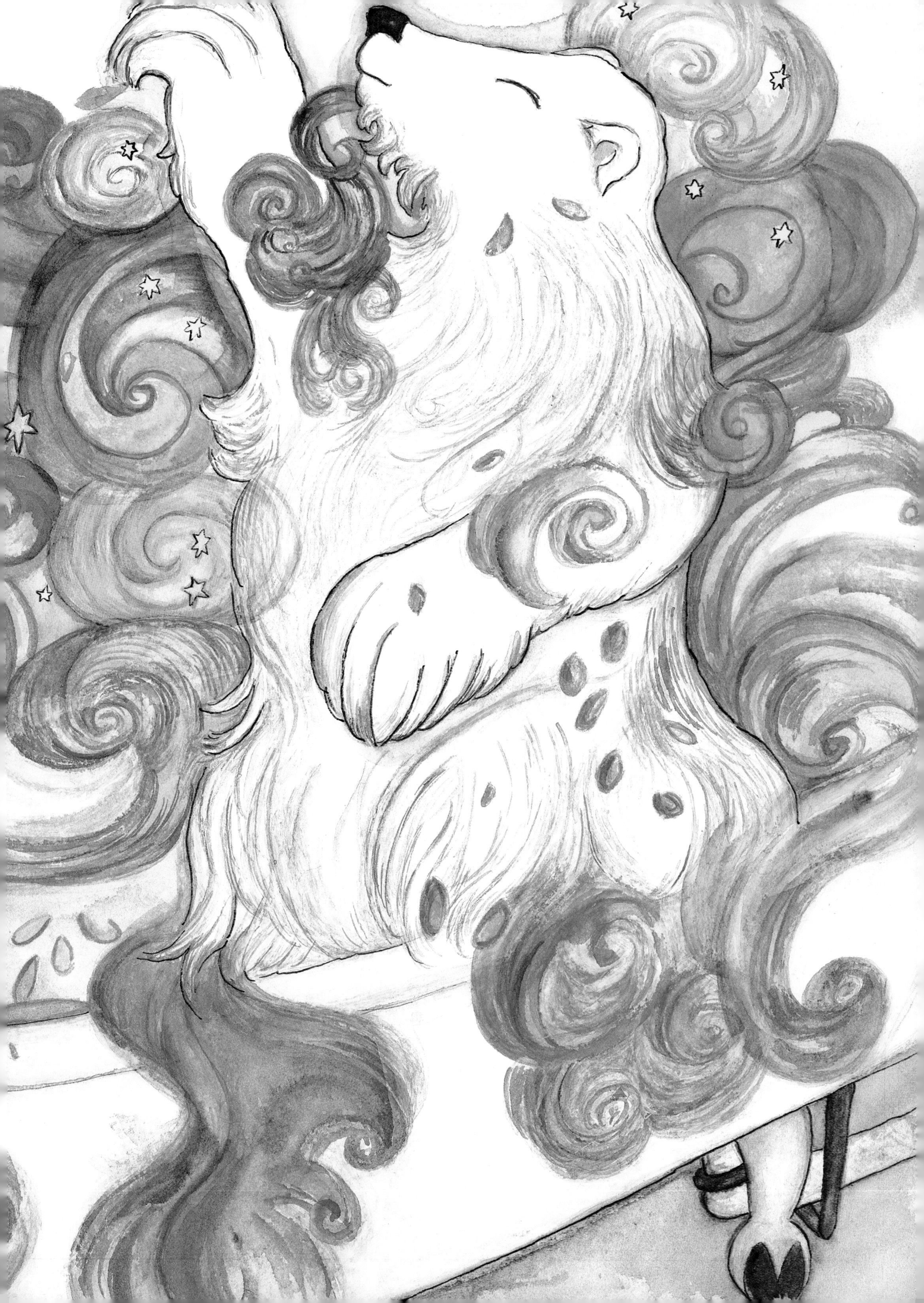

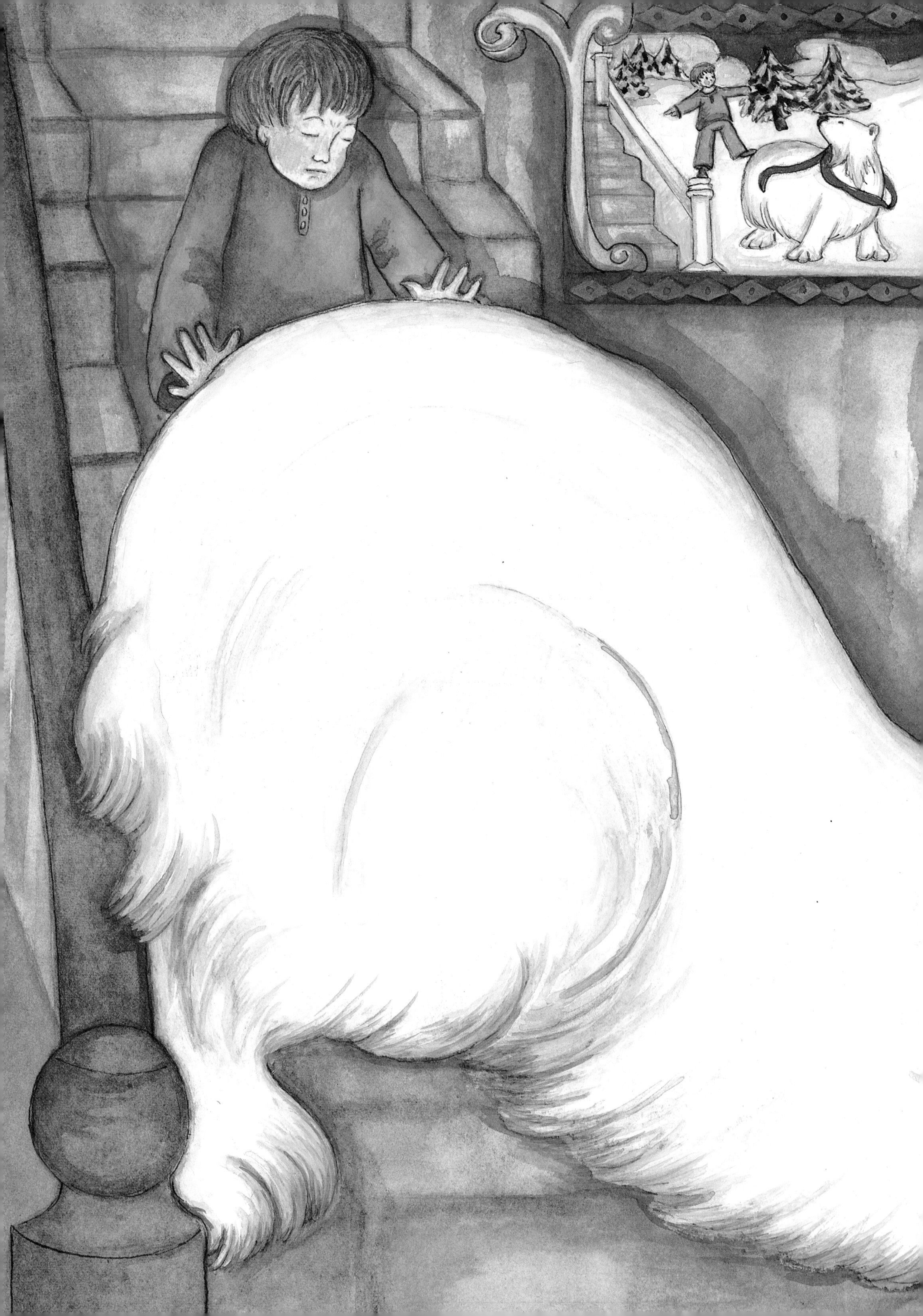

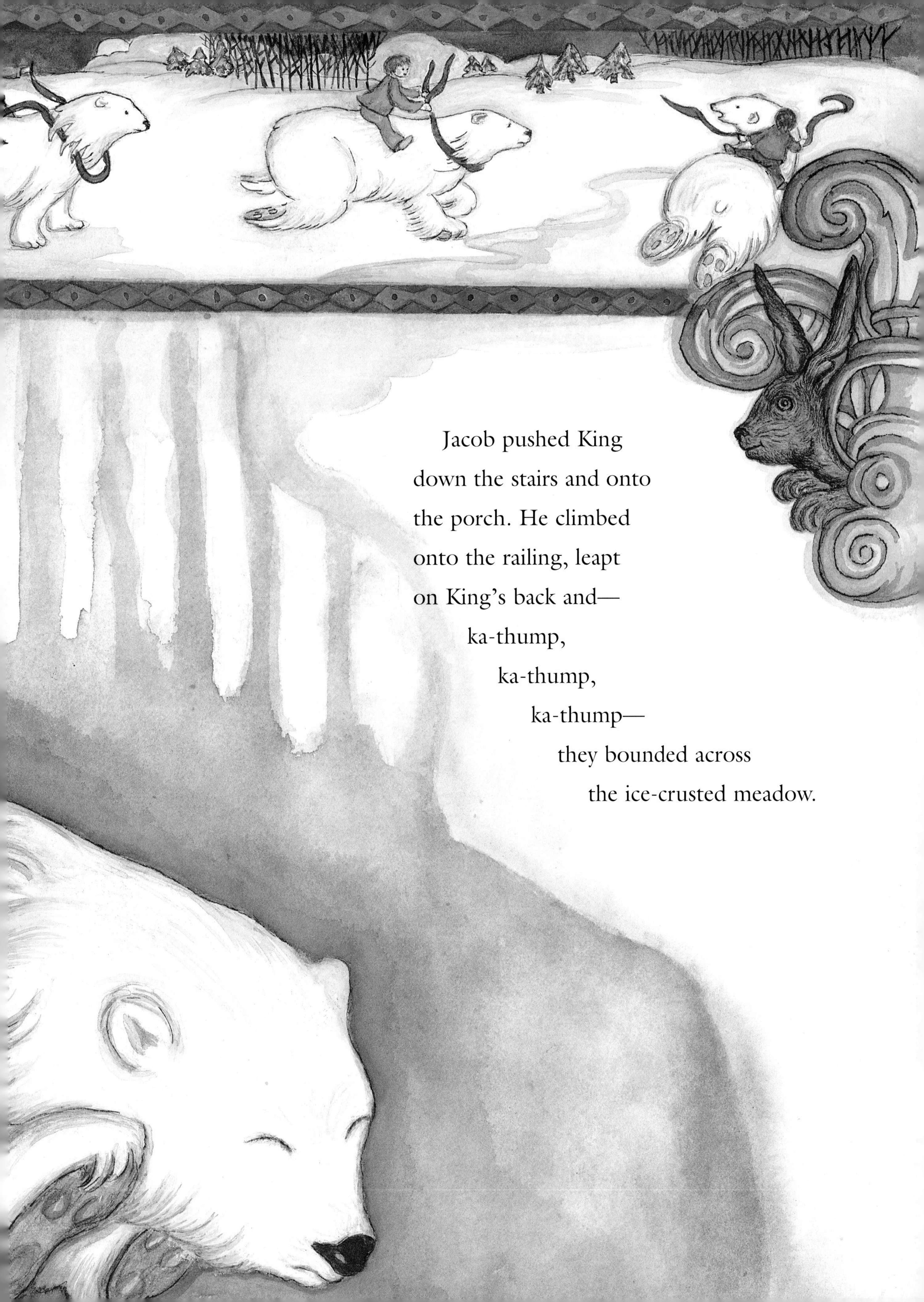

Jacob pushed King
down the stairs and onto
the porch. He climbed
onto the railing, leapt
on King's back and—
ka-thump,
ka-thump,
ka-thump—
they bounded across
the ice-crusted meadow.

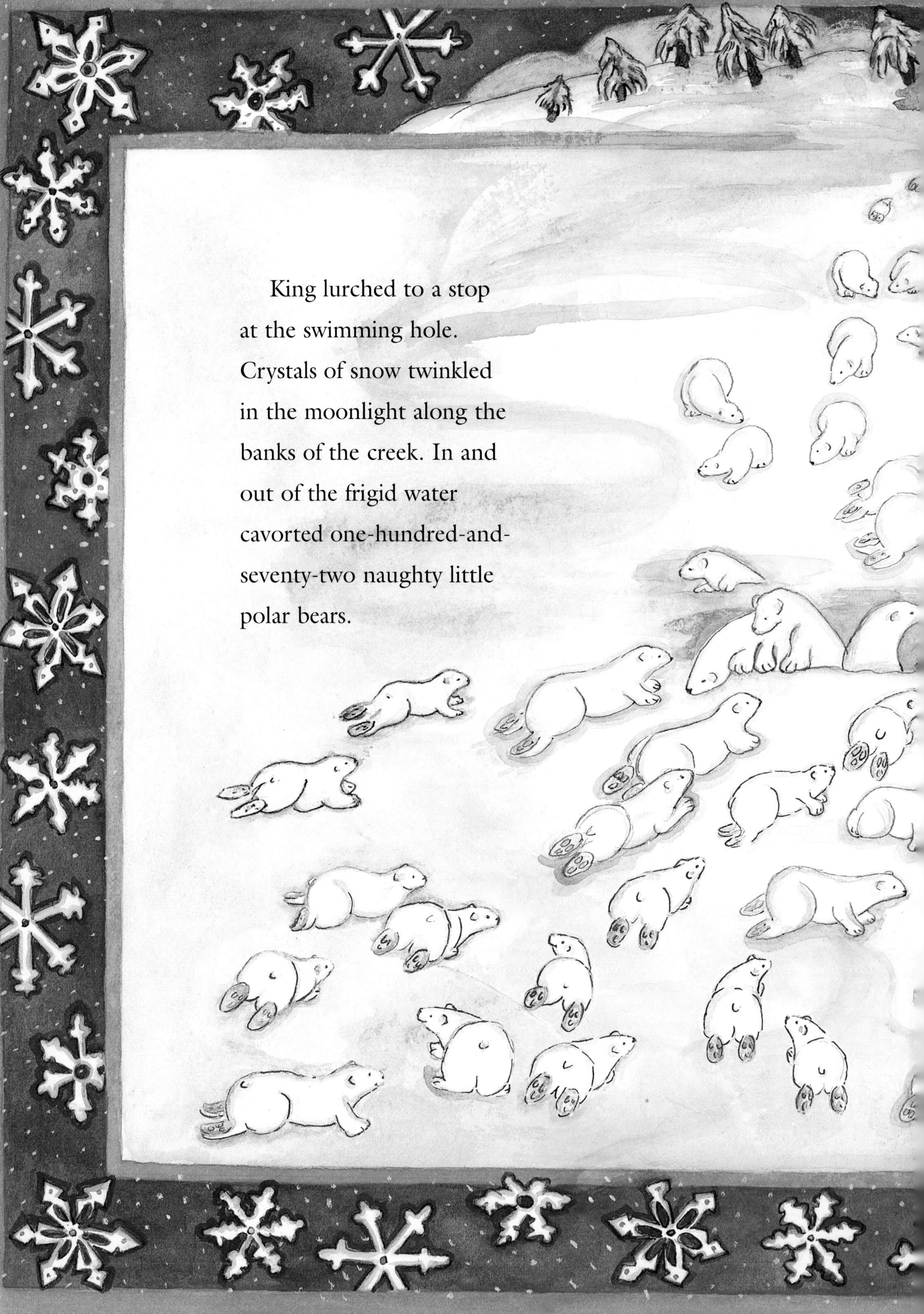

King lurched to a stop at the swimming hole. Crystals of snow twinkled in the moonlight along the banks of the creek. In and out of the frigid water cavorted one-hundred-and-seventy-two naughty little polar bears.

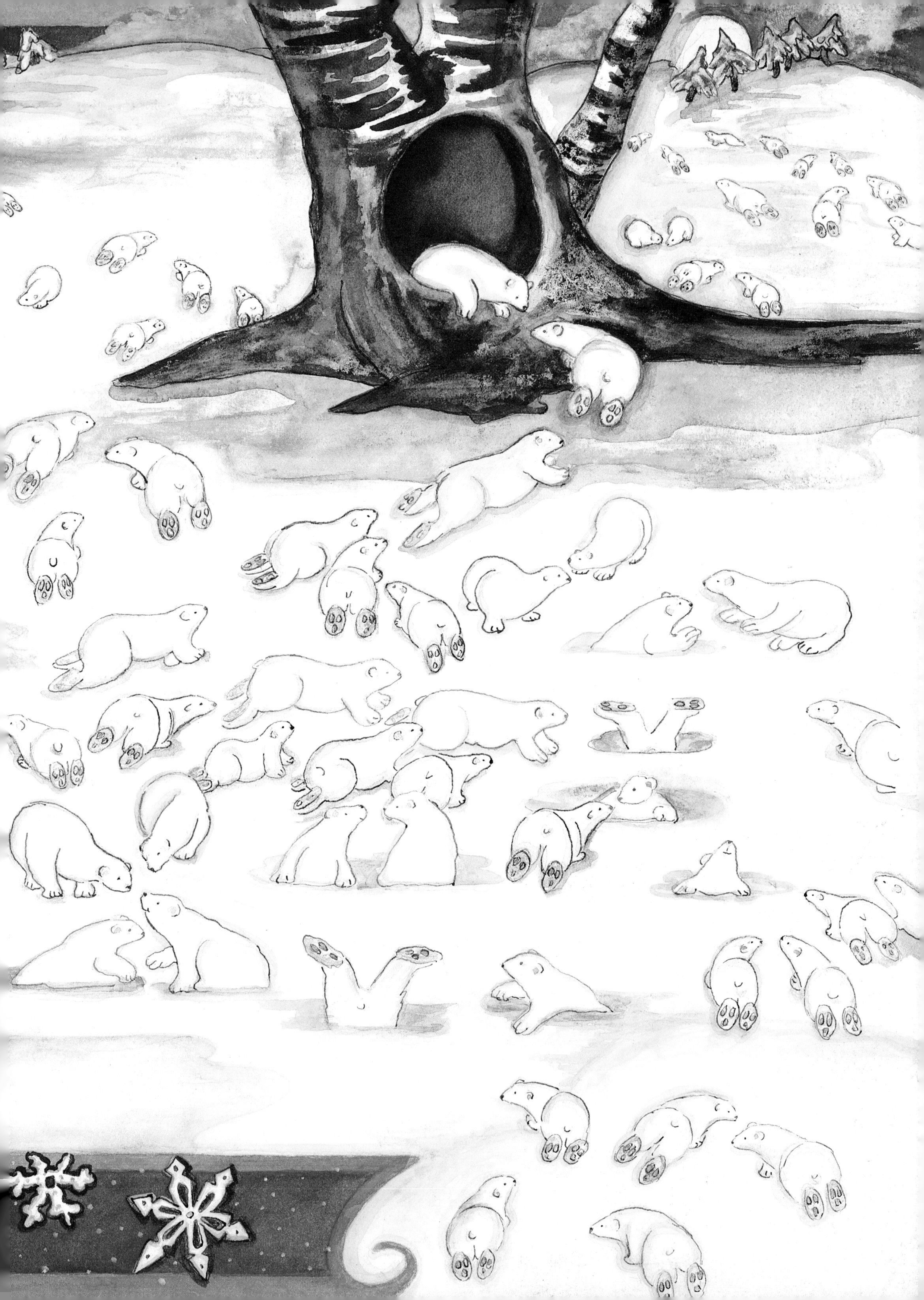

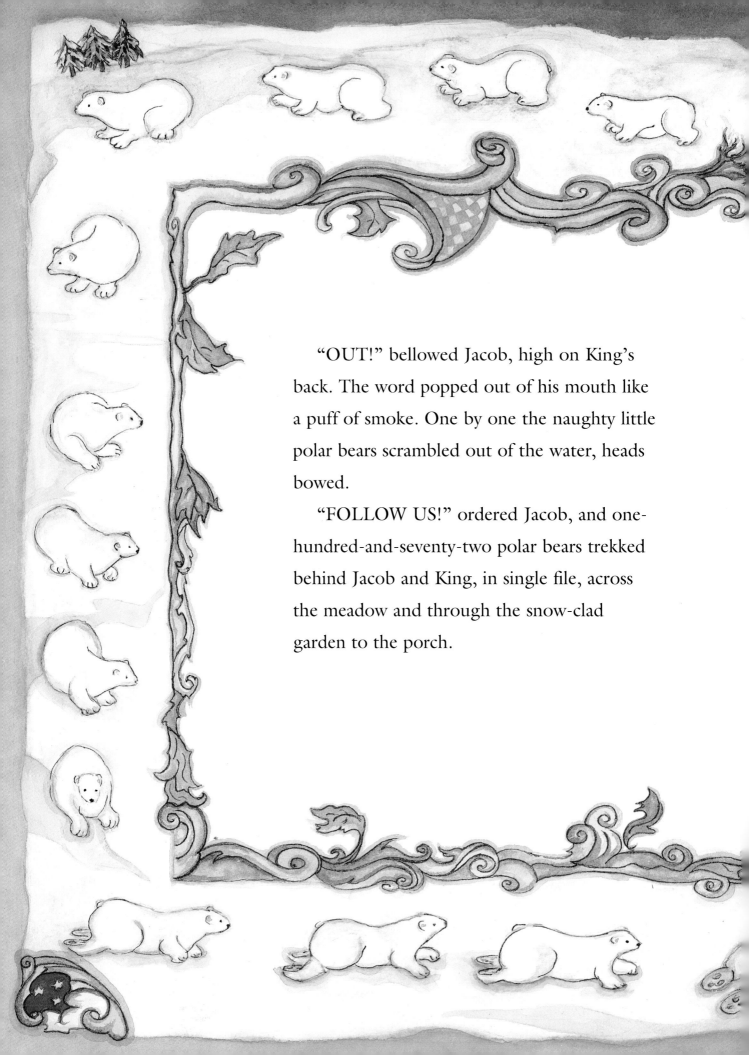

"OUT!" bellowed Jacob, high on King's back. The word popped out of his mouth like a puff of smoke. One by one the naughty little polar bears scrambled out of the water, heads bowed.

"FOLLOW US!" ordered Jacob, and one-hundred-and-seventy-two polar bears trekked behind Jacob and King, in single file, across the meadow and through the snow-clad garden to the porch.

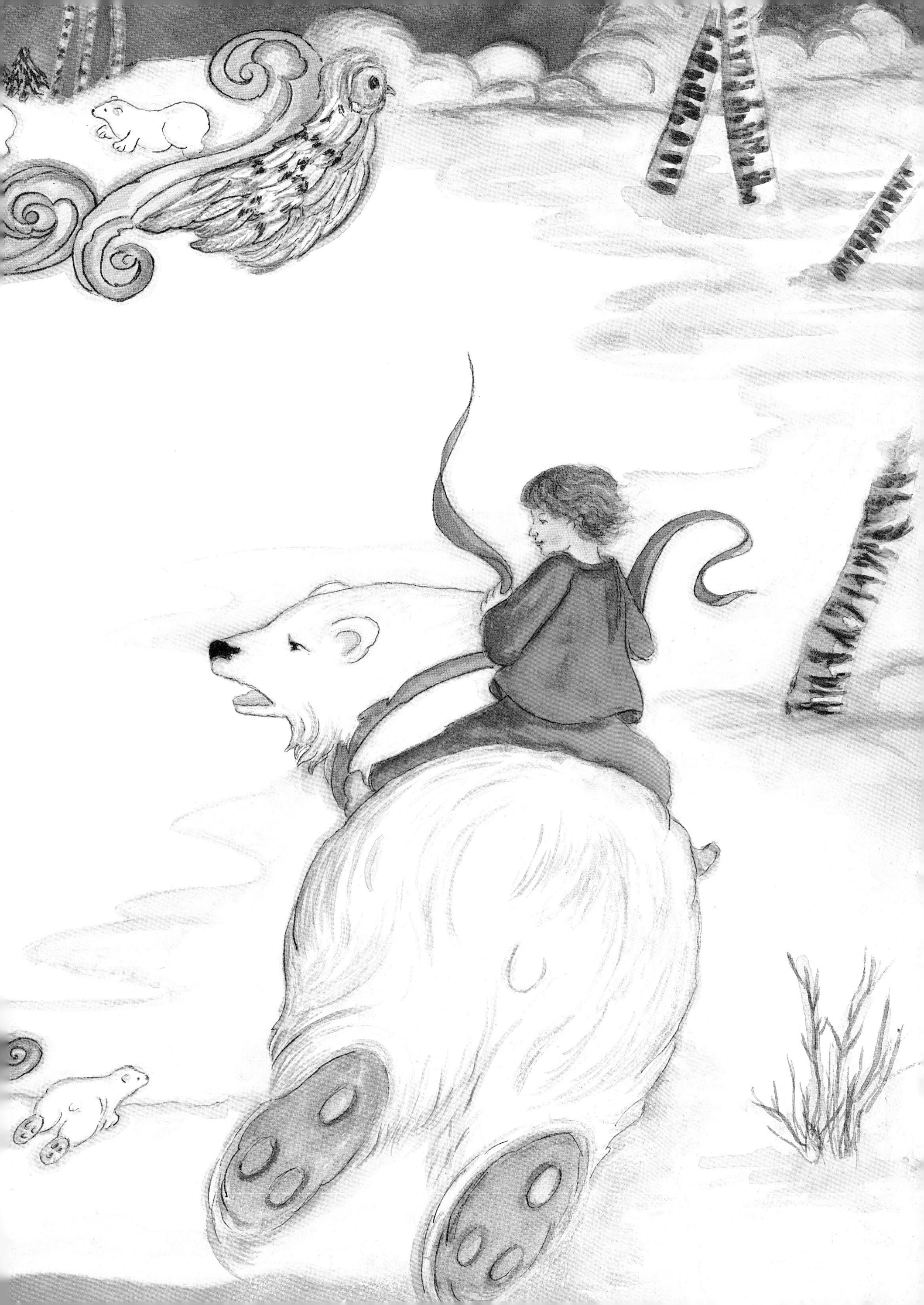

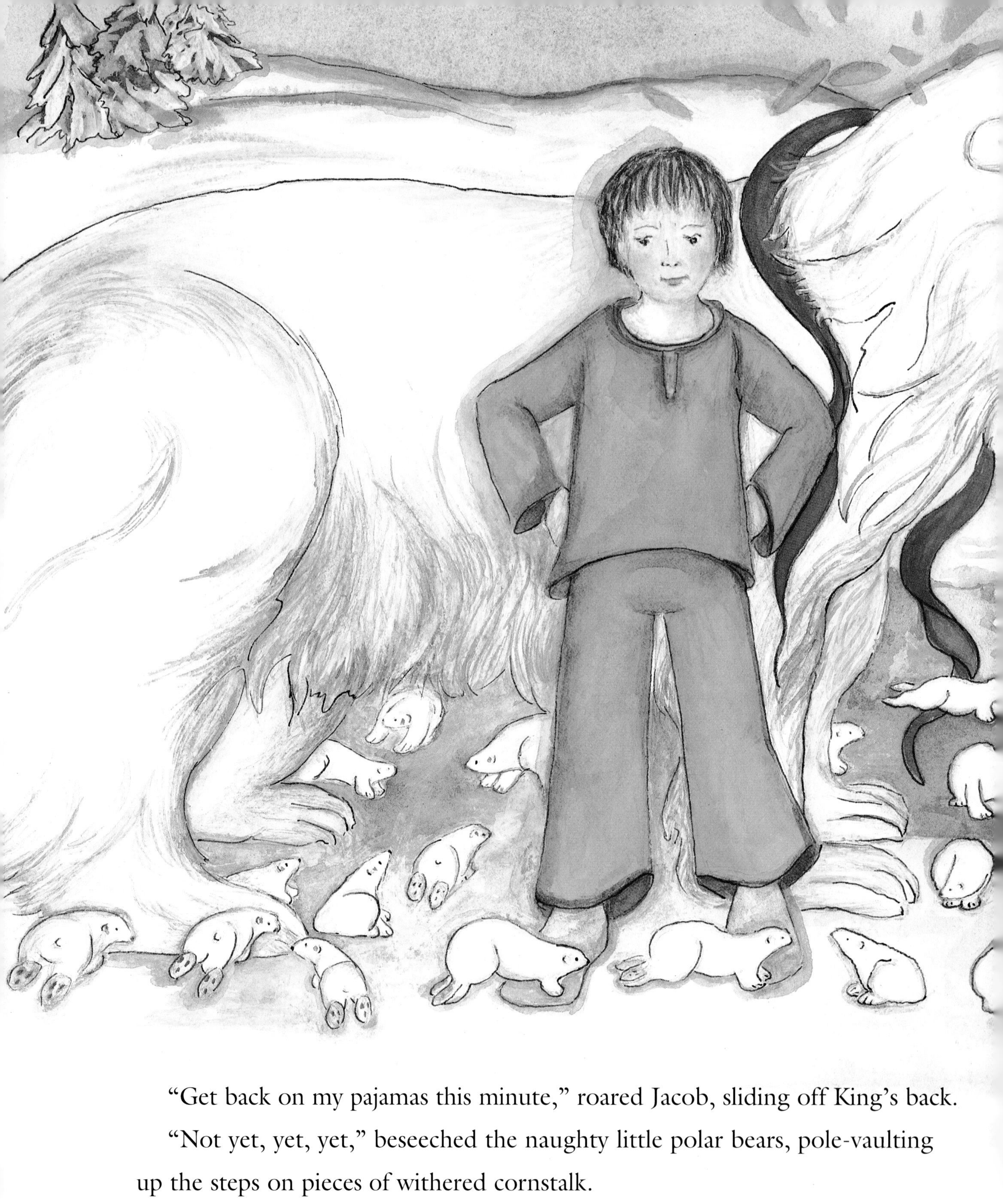

“Get back on my pajamas this minute,” roared Jacob, sliding off King’s back.

“Not yet, yet, yet,” beseeched the naughty little polar bears, pole-vaulting up the steps on pieces of withered cornstalk.

“It’s time for bed,” Jacob said.

“But we want to play, play, play,” the bears squealed, gamboling about Jacob’s feet.

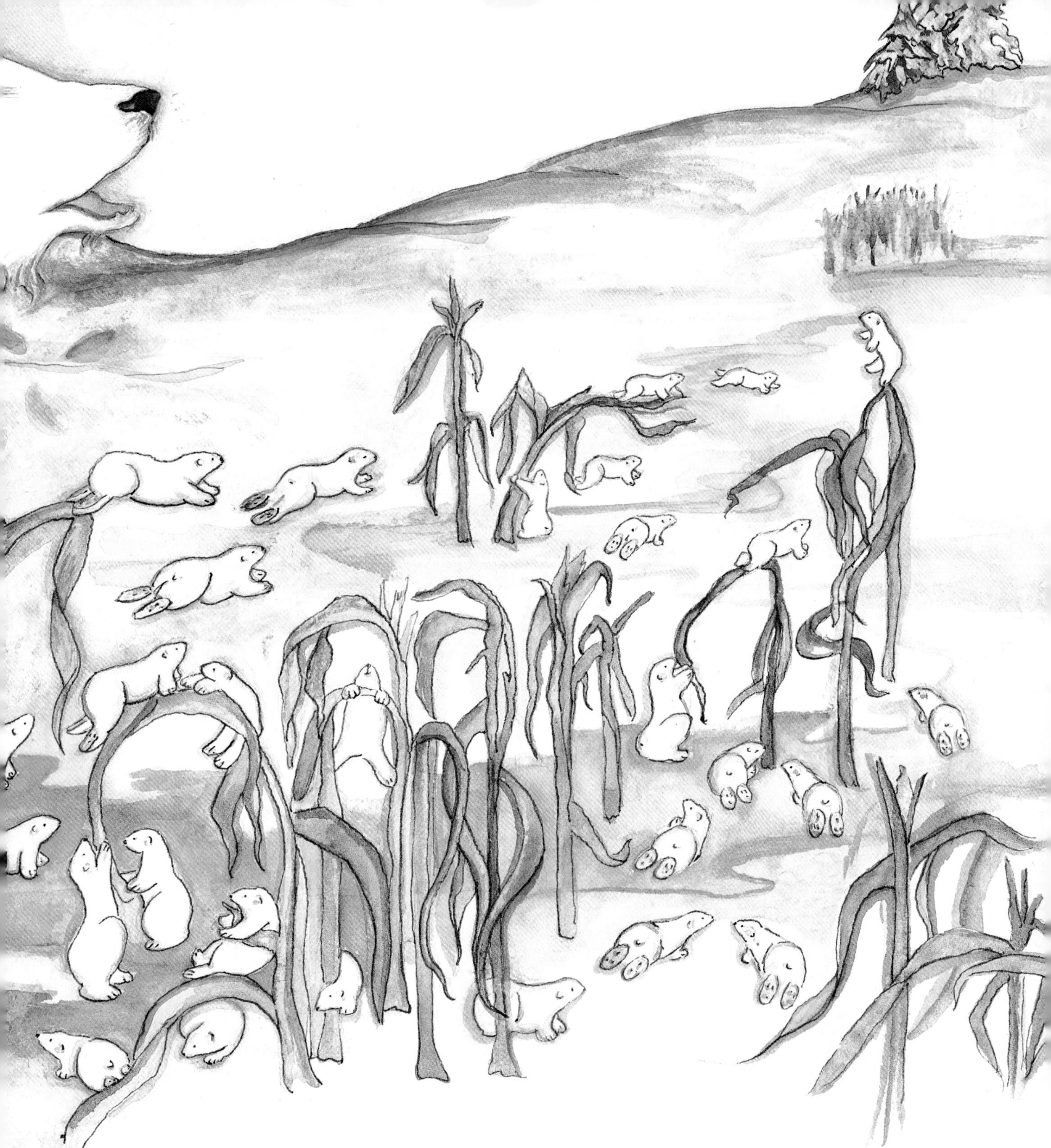

King shook his massive head, and drops of water sprayed all over Jacob and the one-hundred-and-seventy-two naughty little polar bears.

"I've got it!" Jacob clapped his hands. "The perfect place."

"Whee, whee, whee," piped the bears.

"Follow me," said Jacob.

Jacob skipped up the stairs; King lumbered up the stairs; one-hundred-and-seventy-two bears clawed up the stairs and into the bathroom. The tub was almost empty. Jacob turned on the cold water. King nudged Jacob aside and slid one massive leg over the side of the tub.

"Hold on! It's not your turn," said Jacob.

"No, no, no," squeaked the naughty little polar bears.

But King was already jammed into the tub.

Glug, glug, glug, King began to shrink. And shrivel. And sink. In seconds he had disappeared beneath the water.

"Aha," laughed Jacob, scooping out the stuffed bear. "What a clever old King you are." He laid him on top of the hamper to dry.

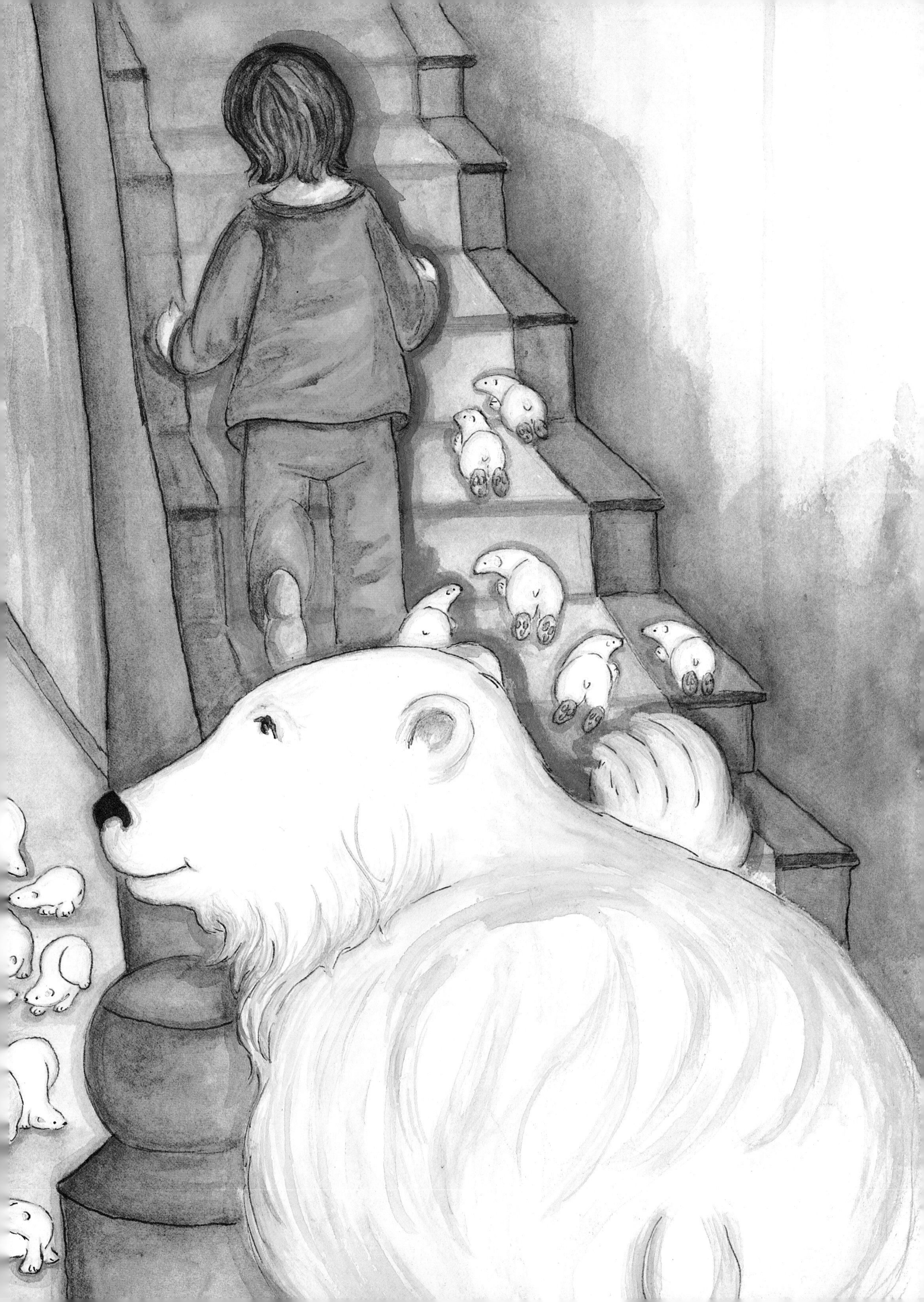

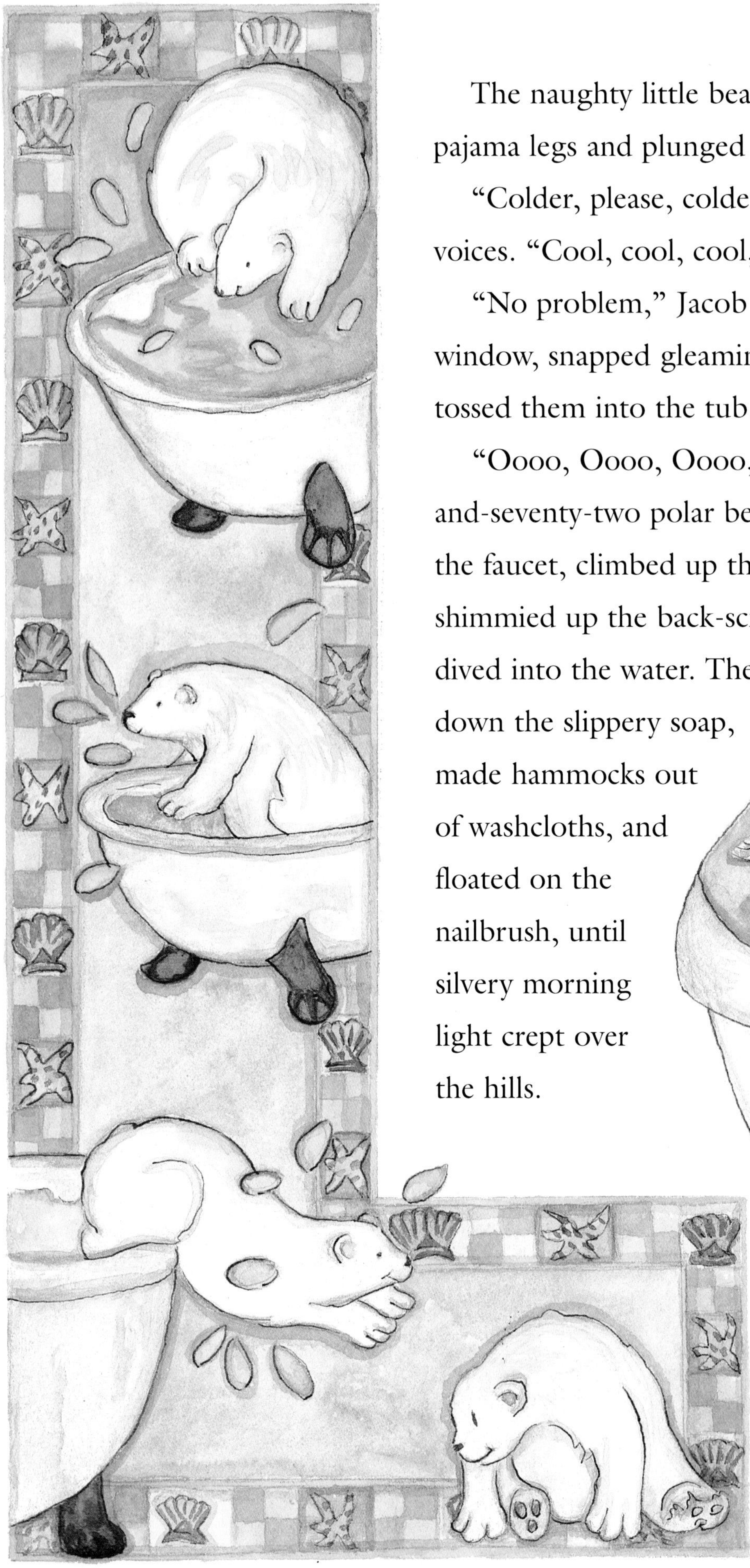

The naughty little bears darted up Jacob's pajama legs and plunged into the water.

"Colder, please, colder," they begged in silly voices. "Cool, cool, cool, like the pool, pool, pool."

"No problem," Jacob said. He opened the window, snapped gleaming icicles off the roof, and tossed them into the tub.

"Oooo, Oooo, Oooo," crooned one-hundred-and-seventy-two polar bears. They clambered up the faucet, climbed up the shampoo bottle, shimmied up the back-scrubber, and dived into the water. They slid down the slippery soap, made hammocks out of washcloths, and floated on the nailbrush, until silvery morning light crept over the hills.

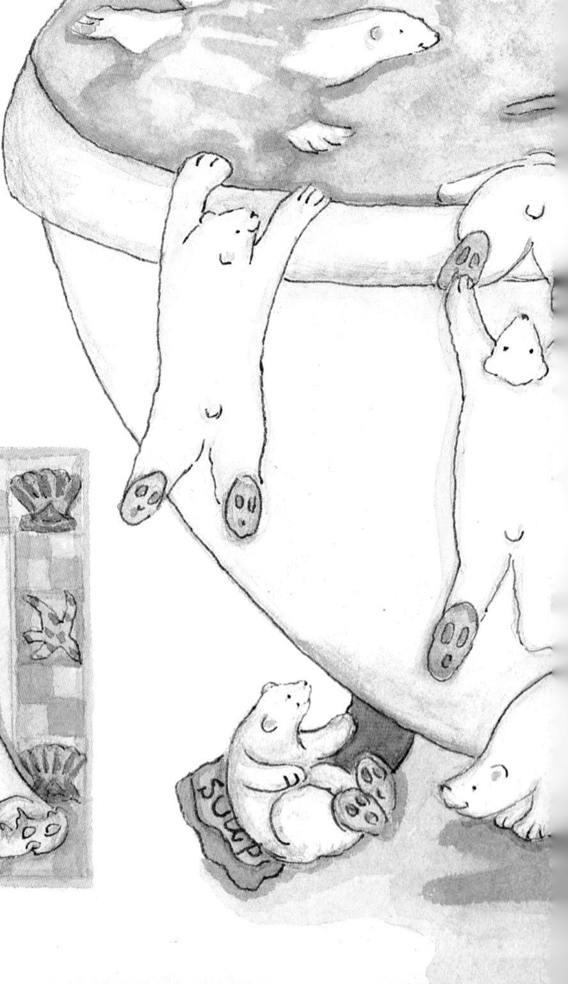
SOAP

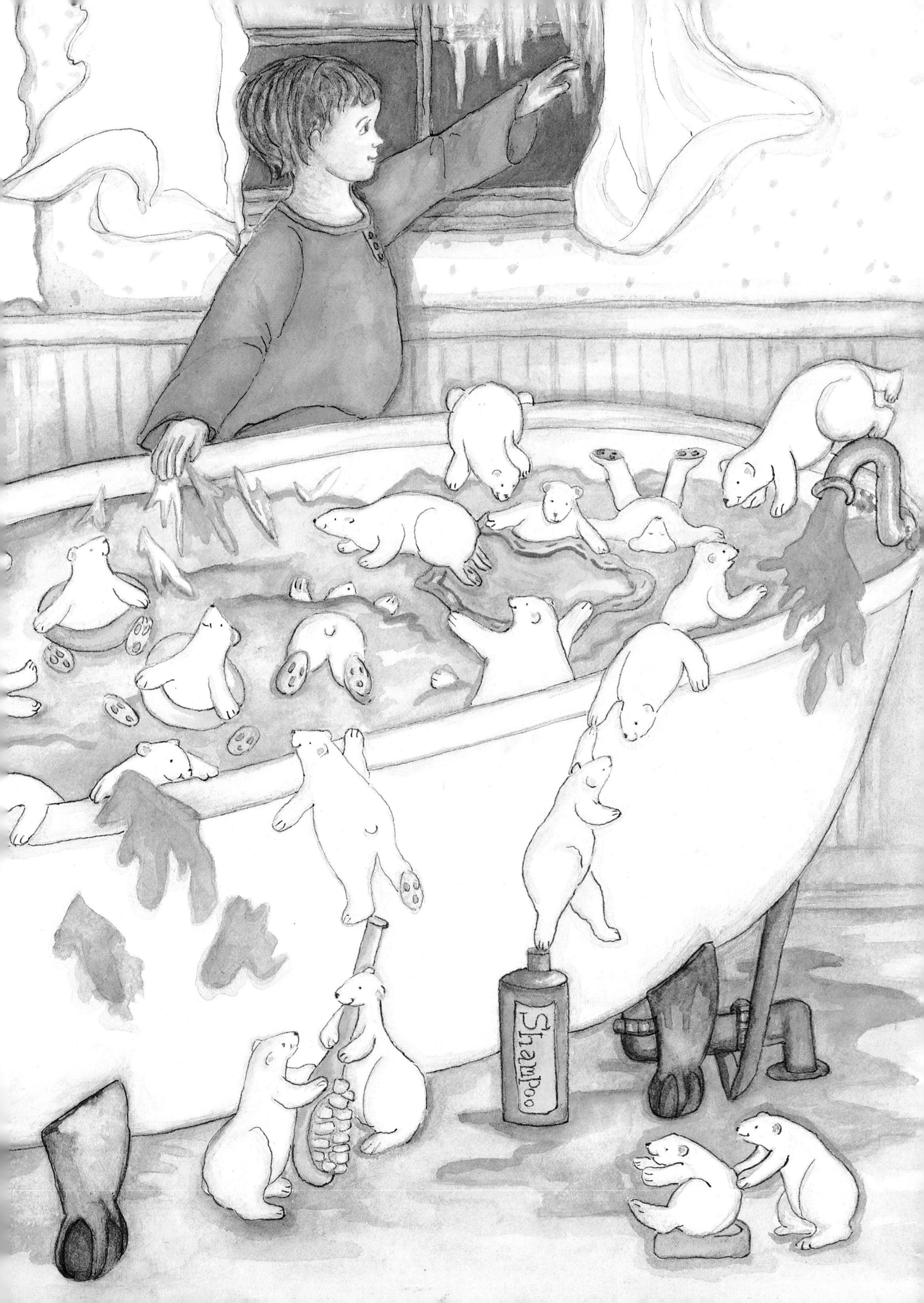
ShamPoo

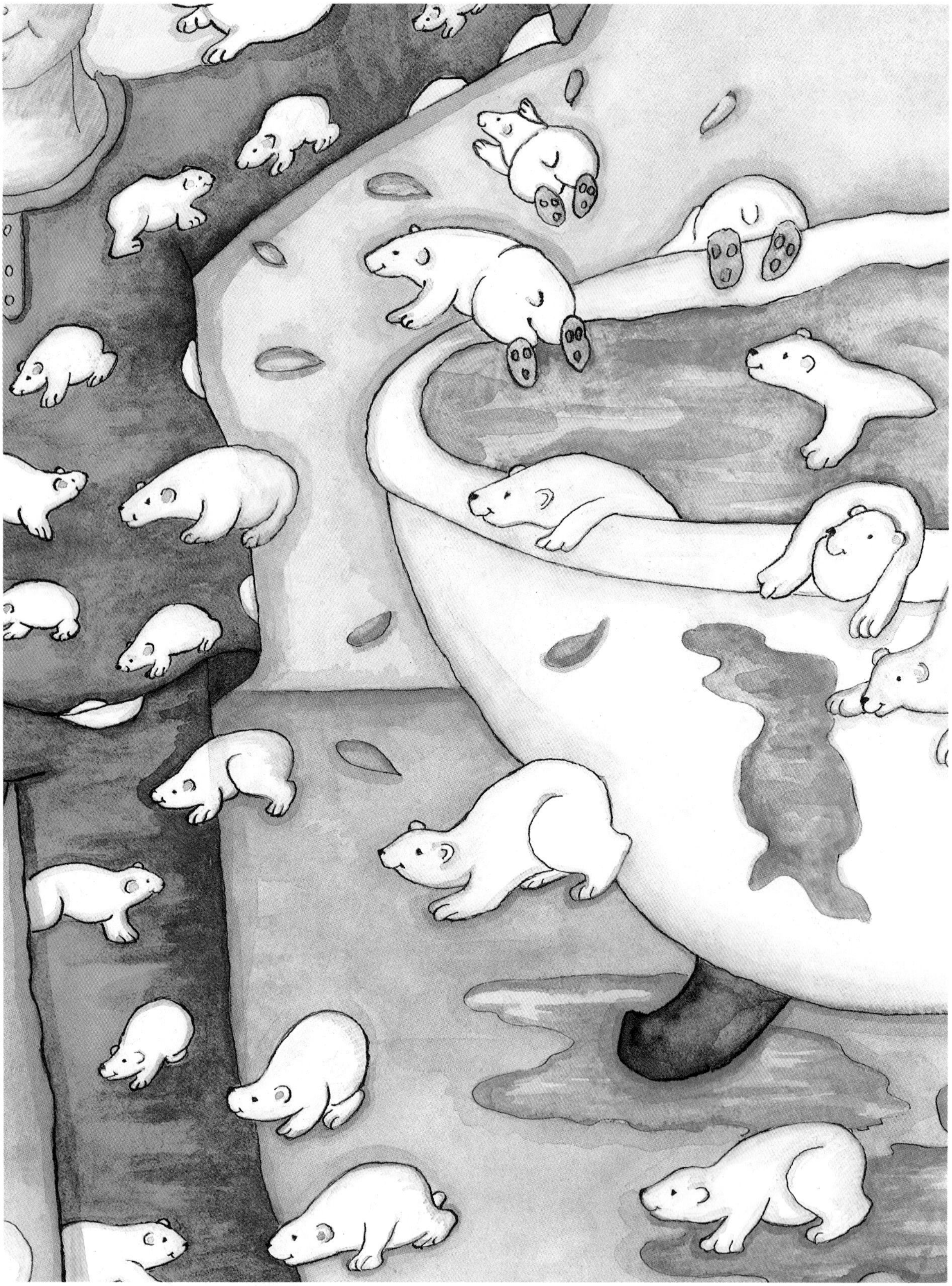

"Bed," begged a weary Jacob.

"Okay, okay, okay." And one-hundred-and-seventy-two little polar bears leapt out of the bathtub and onto Jacob's plain green pajamas until they weren't plain anymore. Jacob tucked King under his arm and toppled into bed.

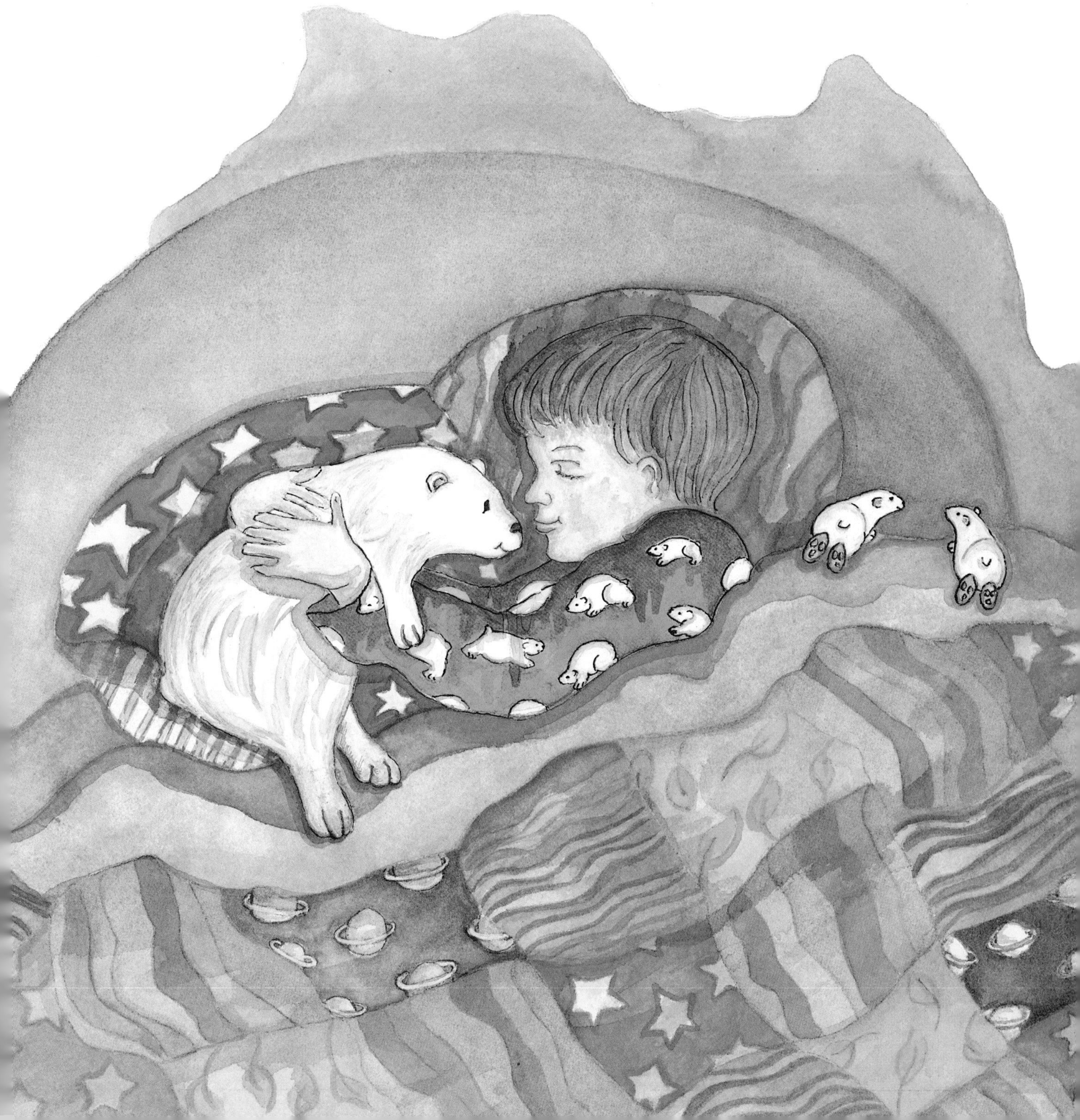

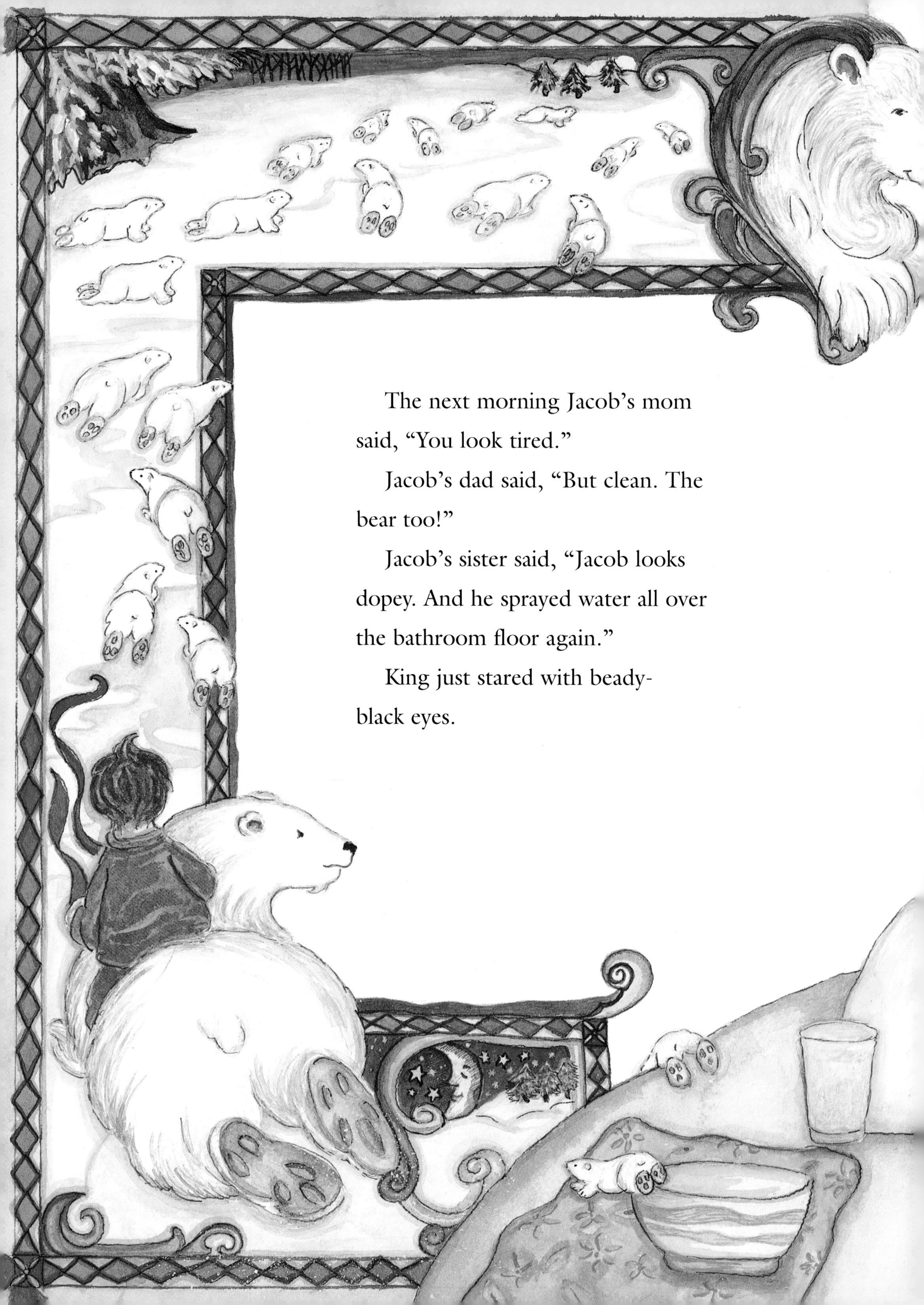

The next morning Jacob's mom said, "You look tired."

Jacob's dad said, "But clean. The bear too!"

Jacob's sister said, "Jacob looks dopey. And he sprayed water all over the bathroom floor again."

King just stared with beady-black eyes.

Jacob chewed his buckwheat pancakes and smiled at his very special, good-as-new pajamas, decorated with one-hundred-and-seventy-two very white polar bears.

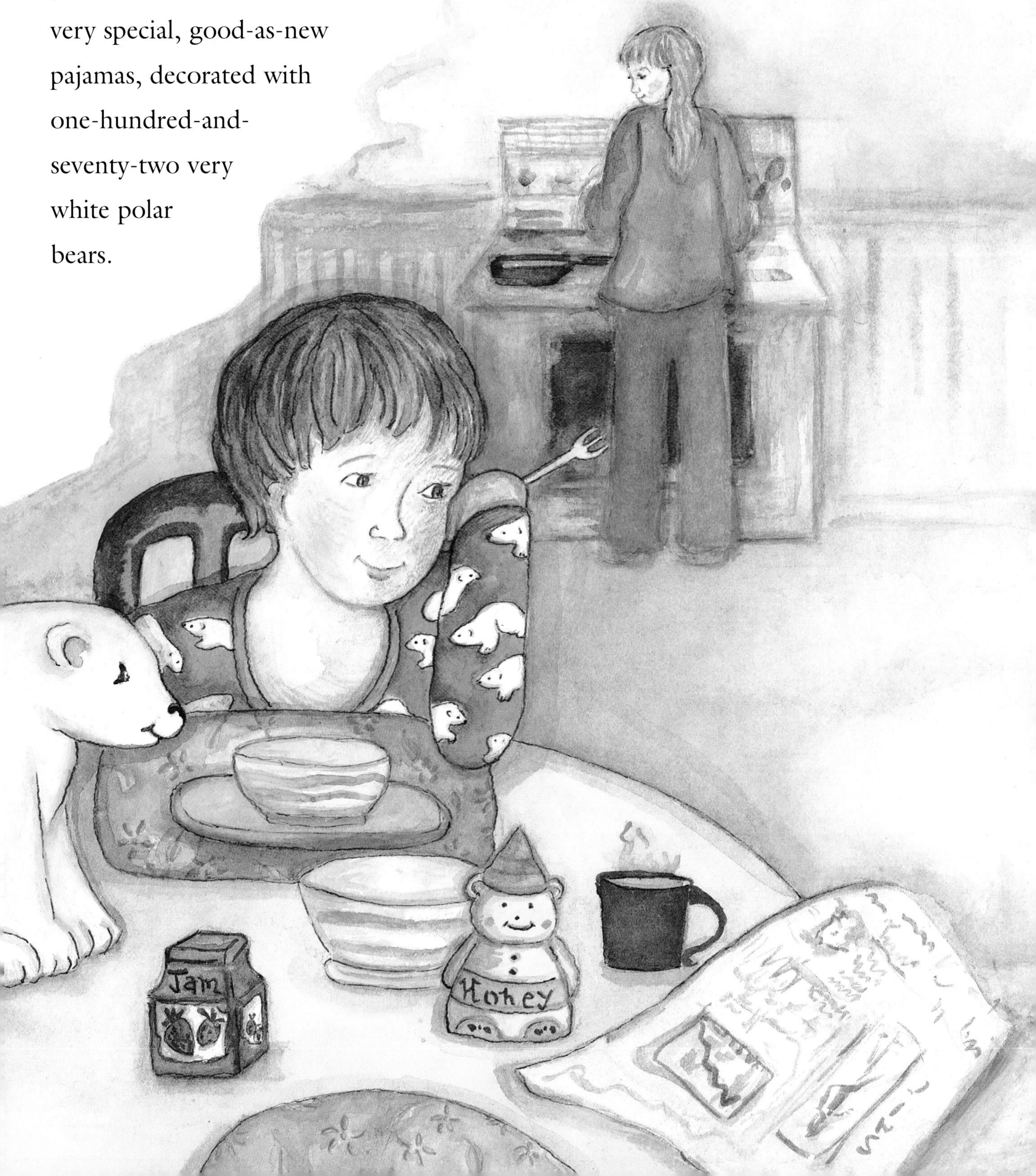
Jam
Honey

The End